J FIC
Selfors, Suzanne.
Hero training : a destiny do-
over diary
2015.

JUL - - 2015

HERO
TRAINING

A DESTINY DO-OVER DIARY

THIS BOOK
BELONGS TO

_____

HERO TRAINING

A DESTINY DO-OVER DIARY

Suzanne Selfors

LB

LITTLE, BROWN AND COMPANY

New York   Boston

Little, Brown and Company

Hachette Book Group
1290 Avenue of the Americas, New York, NY 10104
Visit us at lb-kids.com

Little, Brown and Company is a division of Hachette Book Group, Inc.
The Little, Brown name and logo are trademarks of Hachette Book Group, Inc.

The publisher is not responsible for websites (or their content) that are not owned by the publisher.

First Edition: July 2015

Library of Congress Control Number: 2015935137

ISBN 978-0-316-40139-5

10 9 8 7 6 5 4 3 2 1

RRD-C

Printed in the United States of America

Ever After
Royals!

Headmaster
Grimm

Ever After
Rebels

Dear students,

I am pleased to see that so many of you have registered for Ever After High's prestigious Hero Training class. Your parents and I are delighted that you're embracing your destinies as future storybook heroes. This class is an important step in that honorable direction.

In this beginner course, you will focus on horsemanship, athletic prowess, and the knightly arts. You have the privilege of being taught by Professor Knight himself, a decorated and award-winning expert on the subject.

On another note, as you may have heard, one of your classmates at Ever After High has launched a petition to bring to light the unfair treatment of beasts. You may notice flyers all over the school and videos on the Mirrornet. The Board of Storytellers and I will take this petition under serious consideration. While trying to maintain a strong sense of tradition, we recognize that times do change.

In the meantime, do not let this matter distract you from the task at hand—to become the best, brightest, and bravest heroes of your generation.

Headmaster Grimm

PETITION: EQUAL RIGHTS FOR BEASTS!
Submitted to Headmaster Grimm and the Ever After High Board of Storytellers

DEAR HEADMASTER GRIMM, SCHOOL BOARD, AND ANYONE ELSE UNEASY WITH CHANGE,

My name is Rosabella Beauty, and I am a student at Ever After High. It has come to my attention that the beasts in our village are not always welcome. Ogres are kicked out of cafés. Goblins get glared at while at the Village Mall. Seriously? That is so last chapter.

It's time to end this inequality.

I want to share with you something from the stories my dad told me from when he was the Beast: True beauty comes from what's inside someone, from heroes and princesses to trolls and big bad wolves. Just because beasts don't look "ordinary" doesn't mean they're not kind.

It's time we turned the page. It's time we joined the modern world!

Please check out my flyers around school and on the Mirrornet.

I request that this unfair situation be remedied as soon as possible.

Sincerely,

Rosabella Beauty

→ LETTER TO STUDENTS ←

Young squires, heed my words,

My name is Professor Knight, and I have spent my life in the service of duty and country. I have traveled the kingdom, fought the fight, protected the weak, and most important, completed the quest. And now I have the honor of being your guide as you begin your training to fulfill your destinies as heroes.

Even though this is a beginner's course, be advised that dangerous situations will arise and courage will be needed. My job is to teach you to master the basic knightly skills so that your face will not be fried by dragon fire, you will not fall whilst scaling a tower, and you will not be embarrassed because you've rescued the wrong damsel.

Warning: Goofing around will not be tolerated. Chain mail wedgies are very uncomfortable and not amusing. Anyone caught engaging in such behavior will be sent to dungeon detention.

Remember, the role of hero is the most important duty in the fairytale world. Never forget that. You have been bestowed with a destiny that others can only dream of. Make us proud.

Dutifully yours,

Professor Knight

FIELD TRIP PERMISSION FORM

Dear parents,

Your noble offspring cannot learn heroic skills if they are always trapped in a classroom. They must venture forth to breathe fresh air, to trample the earth, to ride into the wind. And, ultimately, to face the unknown.

Of course, we will do our best to ensure their safety, but as you know, heroic behavior comes with risk. That is why we ask you to fill out the following form.

I give permission for

.... (offspring's name)

to follow Professor Knight wherever he should lead. (Please note that anyone with a fear of heights, dark places, or storms of epic proportions must provide a note from the school physician in order to be excused.)

I also give permission for

.... (offspring's name)

to wield an ax, a sword, a lance, and any other piece of equipment that Professor Knight requires.

If injury should occur during Hero Training, I give permission for the school's infirmary to stitch, cauterize, and bandage any wounds and to set any broken bones. Treatment will also be given for burns, bruises, and blisters. (Please note that search parties will be arranged for the recovery of missing limbs.)

I certify that my offspring is not allergic to dragons.

....

Signature of parent or guardian

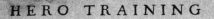

THRONEWORK ASSIGNMENT #1
CHIVALRY HEXERCISE

Chivalry is the code of conduct that a true knight must follow. Though some may think it is old-fashioned, there are many ways to use this code in daily life, even if you aren't a knight in shining armor.

For each chivalrous rule, create a modern example of something a person might do that would represent that rule.

HERO TRAINING

RULE 1: Defend the weak.

RULE 2: Love your kingdom.

RULE 3: Perform your feudal duties.

RULE 4: <u>Respect your king and queen.</u>

RULE 5: Do not lie or go back on your word.

RULE 6: Be generous to everyone.

RULE 7: Always be on the side of right and justice.

DARLING CHARMING WORD SEARCH

Darling Charming is one of the most traditional princesses at Ever After High—at least that's how she appears to be. But in truth, Darling is as strong and heroic as her brothers, Daring and Dexter.

Look for these words that describe Darling in this puzzle. Can you find them all? Words may appear up, down, across, backward, or diagonally! Good luck.

PRINCESS   SLOWS TIME
HEROINE   CHARMING
ELOQUENT   SIR GALLOPAD
ATHLETE   BRAVE
STRONG   SECRETS
RESCUER

```
S U E I D A J E N R P A H E
D T S N G L L K E A R I O T
H C R Z I O Z U W W I L T E
N E V O Q O C V R Y N E X L
M P E U N S R I F M C P J H
N R E U E G L E N B E H K T
J N L R P M M O H I S Q Q A
T S E C R E T S W O S V C O
G N I M R A H C Z S E K X B
M O Z E Z J W B K N T Y A R
S I R G A L L O P A D I S A
Y Q A K A M T S Y M R L M V
G X O U V A B V C E W A W E
X S M X S W P D O X X Z A S
```

THRONEWORK ASSIGNMENT #2
DAMSELS IN DISTRESS QUIZ

Identifying a damsel in distress is a high priority for a hero. Trying to rescue a damsel who is not in distress can have embarrassing results, so it is best to learn which predicaments are considered dire and thus requiring rescue.

1. A princess is locked in a tower and offers you a rope made from her braided hair. You should...

   a. tell her you'll hext her the name of a barbershop because, seriously, that hair is way too long.

   b. climb up and rescue her.

2. A fellow student has to write a paper for Environmental Magic class but hates doing research. You should...

   a. write the paper for her.

   b. invite her to join your study group so she can get help.

HERO TRAINING

3. A fellow student is walking across campus with a piece of 20-feather-ply Princess and the Pea toilet paper stuck to her shoe. You should…

   a. holler at her from across the quad so she can do something about it.

   b. quickly grab it without her noticing, to save her from embarrassment.

4. A runner on the Track and Shield team has tripped and fallen. You reach to help her to her feet, but she insists that she's perfectly capable of getting up on her own. You should…

   a. grab her arm and pull her to her feet anyway because, let's face it, you're the hero.

   b. step back and respect her wishes.

5. A princess is trapped in a dragon's den and is crying for help. You should…

   a. wish her luck.

   b. grab your sword and shield and save her.

Answers: *If you answered b for all the scenarios, congratulations—you are a natural hero. If not, looks like you need more training.*

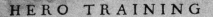

HERO TRAINING

MR. COTTONHORN'S CLOTHES

Every hero needs a trusty companion, and Dexter Charming has Mr. Cottonhorn, a shy jackalope who likes to nibble on fancy miniature thronecakes. He's also quite the snazzy dresser.

Using the art supplies of your choice, can you design some outfits that Mr. Cottonhorn might wear to these two events? Don't forget the accessories!

A fancy banquet at Charming Castle

A picnic in the Enchanted Forest

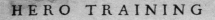

WRITE, IGNITE

Damsels in distress are found in lots of fairytales. Now it's your turn to create a fun story based on this traditional character type.

From the following lists, select your damsel, her predicament, and her hero. If you'd like to leave your choices to chance, roll a die to determine each selection. For example, if you roll a 1, a 5, and a 4, write down *princess, locked in a tower,* and *her best friend forever after.* Then write your story in the space provided on the following pages.

You can do this activity more than once. It will be different every time. Try other combinations!

HERO TRAINING

	Damsel	Predicament	Hero
1.	princess	stuck on a deserted island	herself
2.	cheerhexer	trapped in a dragon's den	a prince
3.	pop star	lost with no money or MirrorPhone	her secret crush
4.	milkmaid	on a terrible blind date	her best friend forever after
5.	sorceress	locked in a tower	a princess
6.	TriCastleOn athlete	on a life raft in the middle of the ocean	create your own hero

RE
Write

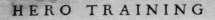

DEXTER'S LOVE POEMS

Dexter Charming is destined to be a hero, but he's also a romantic at heart. He's never had an official girlfriend, but he likes to listen to love songs and write super-sappy poems.

If you think about it, most songs are about love. Secret love. Falling in love. Trying to keep love. Being away from the one you love. And, alas, heartbreak.

Put your playlist on shuffle and listen to five songs.
Write down some of the lyrics that are about love.
What kind of love do they describe? Turn these
romantic lines into your very own charming verse.

Lyrics 1:

Lyrics 2:

Lyrics 3:

Poem 1:

Poem 2:

Poem 3:

Would any of your new poems be useful for Dexter's romantic life? If so, which one?

HERO TRAINING

Perhaps you can think of other poems that would be perfect for the following scenes:

Scene: Dexter is thinking about his secret crush.
Poem:

Scene: Dexter and Raven go on their first date.
Poem:

HEROIC PRINCESS

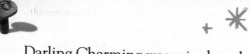

Darling Charming was raised to always act and dress like a perfect fairytale princess. But Darling is strong and courageous. She's determined to be the hero of her own story. And maybe even the hero of other stories, too.

Using the art supplies of your choice, can you create some athletic wear for Darling? Her clothing has to be comfortable so she can run, ride, and work out. But there's no reason why it can't also be stylish.

DEXTER'S DATE

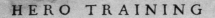

What if Dexter finally worked up the courage to ask Raven on another date? He'd definitely be nervous, and he'd need some help putting together his wardrobe. Using the art supplies of your choice, can you design some outfit options for his date with the Evil Queen's daughter?

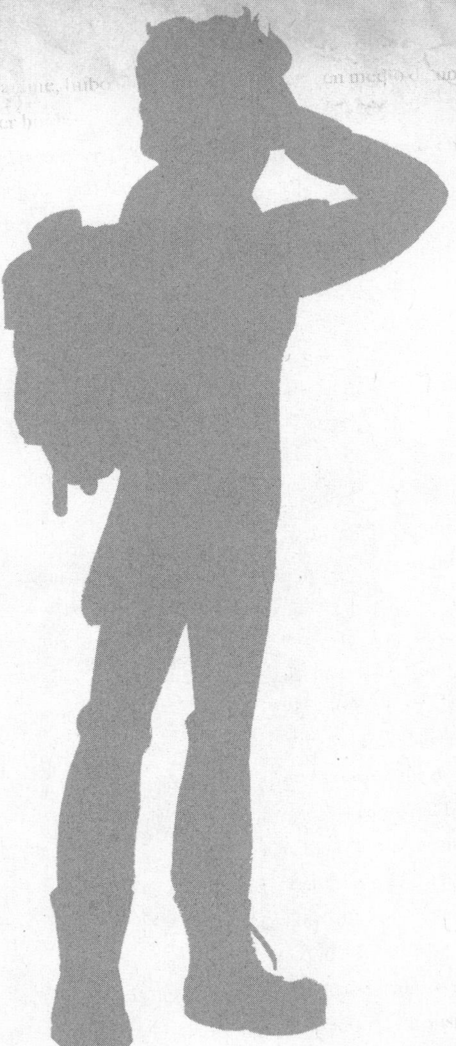

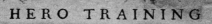

THRONEWORK ASSIGNMENT #3
HEROIC RHYMES

EACH OF THESE SENTENCES IS MISSING SOME WORDS THAT RHYME.

Fill in the blanks with the words provided.

1. To finish the . . . . , you must first pass

   a . . . .

2. To speed up your . . . . , hitch it to

   a . . . .

3. Never lower your . . . . unless you

   wish to . . . .

HERO TRAINING

4. Learn how to use a . . . . by slicing

through a . . . .

5. If you don't have a . . . . to cross the

. . . . , I hope you can . . . .

6. The . . . . will always . . . .

for that which is . . . .

---

yield	test	right
knight	shield	dragon
fight	wagon	float
moat	gourd	sword
quest	boat	

Answers: 1. quest, test; 2. wagon, dragon;
3. shield, yield; 4. sword, gourd; 5. boat, moat,
float; 6. knight, fight, right

45

DARLING'S COAT OF ARMS

A coat of arms is a design that is unique to a family or an individual. A knight in shining armor will often display it on his shield.

The Charming family has a coat of arms, but Darling would love to have her own. Can you create some options for her? Think of things that might represent Darling. Remember that she is beautiful, courageous, and very strong. She loves her horse, Sir Gallopad, and galloping through the woods with him. She likes reading and wearing armor, and she yearns for adventure.

THRONEWORK ASSIGNMENT #4
WHAT IS A HERO?

The word *hero* is used to describe a person who is admired for deeds of bravery and for having noble qualities.

Do you agree with this definition?

Do you have a hero? Maybe he or she is someone you've read about. Or someone you know personally. Are you a hero? You might say no, but think about it. Have you ever helped someone else? Sure you have! Have you ever faced something that you were afraid of? Share the story on the next pages.

My hero is

I am a hero because

GALLANT SIR GALLOPAD

Darling's horse, Sir Gallopad,
is loyal and brave. In the
book *A Semi-Charming Kind
of Life*, he and Darling share
many adventures.

HERO TRAINING

Let's imagine that Darling has been invited to go riding with some of the other princesses. She wants Sir Gallopad to look extra-nice. Using the art supplies of your choice, can you design a saddle and reins for him? Don't forget to decorate his mane and tail. And remember, he has a special magical talent—he can change color, so there's no limit to your color scheme.

HERO TRAINING

The Hero Training class is holding another jousting tournament. Can you design Sir Gallopad's costume for this event? Remember, during a joust, a horse will wear not only a saddle but also armor to protect his head.

EVER AFTER Royals!

REWRITE, IGNITE

In *A Semi-Charming Kind of Life*, Queen Charming tells her daughter: "Pretty is as pretty does."

What does it mean to be pretty? Is it mostly about how you look? Is it mostly about how you act? Or is it what's on the inside that counts?

This is a tough subject! Many girls and boys feel the pressure to look a certain way, which is so unfair. We look in the mirror and criticize ourselves. We want to change things. We focus on what we see as imperfections.

Now, can you imagine a world without mirrors? What if no one cared about makeup or hairstyles or clothing sizes? Draw or write about what really makes you beautiful, what gives you your inner charm.

RE
Write

Can you create a story about a world without mirrors?

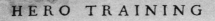

DEXTER CHARMING WORD SEARCH

Can you find these words related to Dexter?
Words may appear up, down, across, backward,
or diagonally!

POETIC   ROMANTIC

UNDERDOG   PRINCE

SECOND BEST   CHARMING

COMIC BOOKS   COMPUTERS

MR. COTTONHORN   SHY

GLASSES   TECH CLUB

```
N D U Y N E I C H S T O T W
I R Q N C C H Z K R S Y J Y
S Q O N D A R O Q B E R L W
A E I H R E O D I R B S H Y
O R S M N B R C E H D L M F
P X I S C O S D N U N E B I
R N V I A S T X O A O Y R A
G B M H D L A T Z G C P O A
Z O N W L Y G X O Y E W M C
C O M P U T E R S C S B A I
A X N R N K B H D K R C N T
J P F G J O T I E I D M T E
B U L C H C E T S W U F I O
F M Z V V D N B E N K M C P
```

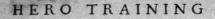

PETITION TO END BEAST INEQUALITY

Rosabella Beauty needs your help. She's been very busy with all her causes, such as trying to get the Castleteria to serve only food that hasn't been magically modified and working hard on rights for beasts. She believes that girls, boys, and beasts have the right to eat in cafés, receive citizenship, and vote.

Can you help Rosabella write her petition?

Dear Headmaster Grimm,

Signed,

Rosabella Beauty

WHAT KIND OF HERO ARE YOU?

TAKE THIS QUIZ TO FIND OUT
WHERE YOU FALL ON THE EVER
AFTER HIGH HERO SCALE.

1. A huge rainstorm has hit your town, and the
   roads are flooded. You...
   a. borrow your neighbor's spellboat and zip
   around town, delivering people to shelter.
   b. advise people to wait on their roofs for help.
   c. lie on your roof and try to get a tan.

2. An elderly blind man doesn't realize that the
   crosswalk lights and bells have stopped
   working. You...
   a. take his arm and help him across the street.

b. inform him that there's a working light a few blocks away.

c. check your MirrorPhone to see if you can hext someone for advice.

---

4. A toddler is running from her mother straight toward a busy road! You...

a. grab her before she steps off the sidewalk.

b. call out to her mom.

c. wave one arm at the traffic as you try not to spill your latte.

---

5. A cat is stuck up a tree. You...

a. grab your tower-climbing gear, which you keep nearby at all times, and shimmy up that tree, catch the cat, and return it to its happy owner.

b. call the fire department.

c. walk past the tree toward the mall because you really need new shoes.

Answers: Time to add up your answers and find out if you're a hero!
Mostly a's: Congratulations! You are definitely Ever After High hero material.
Mostly b's: You are more comfortable directing than taking action, which might make you a hero in some situations but a bystander in others.
Mostly c's: Fairy-fail! Seriously?! Why did you even take this quiz?!

MOAT MAYHEM

Poor Dexter. Hero Training didn't go so well today. The squires had to swim across a moat that was filled with all sorts of dangerous things, including crocodiles, poisonous frogs, and electric eels. Dexter knows how to swim, but he doesn't have prescription swimming goggles, so he ran into all sorts of trouble.

Can you help Dexter find his way through the moat?

START HERE

FINISH

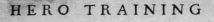

DEAR DIARY
✳ DEXTER ✳

In *A Semi-Charming Kind of Life*, Dexter puts on his armor and starts sneezing. He worries that he might be allergic to armor. That would be a terrible situation because a knight in shining armor is one of the traditional heroic roles—and Dexter is destined to be a hero.

Can you think of something else Dexter might be allergic to? Something that might make it difficult for him to be a hero? For instance, what if he was allergic to horses or to swords? What if he was allergic to damsels?

Imagine that on the day Dexter discovers this new allergy, he sits down and writes an entry in his diary. It's your turn to be the storyteller. What does Dexter write?

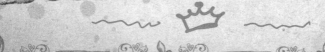

Dear Diary,

HERO TRAINING

ARE YOU A DAMSEL IN DISTRESS?

A distressed damsel is a young lady who finds herself in a dire predicament. According to tradition, she cannot help herself. Rather, she must wait to be rescued.

Take the following quiz to find out if you are a distressed damsel.

1. Your town is in the middle of a heat wave and the air-conditioning in your bedroom is broken. You...
   a. learn how to fix the AC unit yourself.
   b. go to the store and buy a fan.
   c. sit quietly and wait for someone to fix it.

2. Your dog is missing. You...
   a. call all your friends and lead a search party.
   b. make posters and put them up all over town.
   c. sit on the porch and wait for someone to bring your dog back.

3. You've been elected president of the Royal Student Council, but you've never given a speech and you're feeling anxious. You...
   a. ask the theater teacher for some helpful tips.
   b. practice your speech in front of family and friends.
   c. don't write a speech but hope that the vice president comes to your rescue.

4. Your wicked stepmother locks you in a tower. You...
   a. tie the bedsheets together and climb out.
   b. pick the lock on the door and set yourself free.
   c. wait. And wait. And...by now you should know the routine.

Answers: If you answered anything but c, good for you! You are not a distressed damsel! If you answered c, then you will fit in perfectly in Ever After High's Damsel-In-Distressing class.

HERO HEXTBOOK

Professor Knight is writing a hextbook for his class, Hero Training. But he got caught in a rainstorm and his suit of armor rusted, so he's having trouble finishing. Can you help him by filling in some of the chapters?

HERO TRAINING

CONTENTS

MENTOR MAGIC

In *A Semi-Charming Kind of Life*, Madam Maid Marian acts as a mentor to Darling Charming. What does that mean, exactly? A mentor is a wise and trusted counselor or teacher—in other words, someone we look up to or someone who helps guide us in a particular skill or teaches us life lessons. We learn, grow, and prosper thanks to our mentor's nurturing. Madam Maid Marian encourages Darling to embrace her true destiny as a hero.

Do you have a mentor? You might say no, but if you think long and hard, there's likely someone who taught you how to do something or encouraged you to try new things.

Can you write about your mentor? After you're finished, consider sharing your story with him or her.

HATS FOR MADAM MAID MARIAN

Madam Maid Marian teaches the Damsel-In-Distressing class at Ever After High. While teaching the class, she tries to look like a traditional princess by wearing a headdress shaped like a cone. The hat is weird—no doubt about it—but that's what princesses wore in the days when knights galloped around in armor and castles were surrounded by crocodile-infested moats.

Using the art supplies of your choice, can you design cone hats for Madam Maid Marian to wear? Create one for each season.

summer

fall

winter

spring

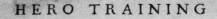

♥ LETTERS OF LOVE ♥

Being the only girl in the Charming family, Darling receives many letters, gifts, and other romantic gestures from boys all across the kingdom. She is destined to be a princess, and marrying her guarantees them the role of a famous Charming prince.

But sometimes these boys write the silliest letters. They can't help themselves. Their brains are muddled with emotions.

Can you write some of the funny love letters that Darling might receive?

Dearest Darling,

Bob, the boy next door

Dearest Darling,

Stinky the ogre

Dearest Darling, ♡

Humphrey Dumpty

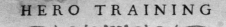

Dexter Charming has been crushing on Raven Queen ever since he met her. But he's too shy to tell her how he feels. If Dexter got the courage to write a love letter to Raven, what might he say?

Dearest Raven,

Dexter Charming

Now write a letter to a friend or to someone you might be crushing on.

BEDTIME STORIES FOR A JACKALOPE

Mr. Cottonhorn is not the typical hero's pet. He's a bit shy, and one of his favorite activities is to visit Ever After High's grand library. Then, after Dexter helps him check out a stack of books, he likes to snuggle in bed and read a bedtime story. But watch out for those antlers! They're pretty sharp!

Do you have any bedtime stories that you'd recommend for Mr. Cottonhorn? Write the titles on the next page.

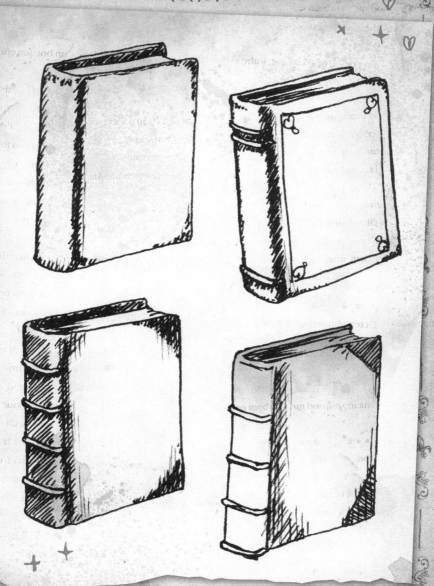

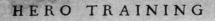

DAMSEL HEXTBOOK

Madam Maid Marian has been asked to write a hextbook for Damsel-In-Distressing. She's nervous about being published, but now that she's no longer stealing from the rich, she sure could use the extra money. However, she needs some help coming up with the chapter titles.

DAMSEL-IN-DISTRESSING

CONTENTS

QUEEN CHARMING'S LADYLIKE LIST

Queen Charming has tried to raise her only daughter, Darling, to be a perfect princess. The queen created the following list to help her daughter remember the strict rules of behavior. Some of these rules seem very outdated and ridiculous, but some are simply good manners that everyone could follow.

Circle the rules that you think you should use in your everyday life. Cross out the ones that are silly.

Rules for Perfect Princesses ♡

BY HER ROYAL MAJESTY QUEEN CHARMING

1. Always keep a smile on your face.
2. Never say mean-spirited things about other people.
3. Never run. Always glide.
4. Never burp at the table.
5. Never use the word *bathroom*. Always say *powder room* or *ladies' room*.
6. Always say *please* and *thank you*.
7. Always curtsy when being introduced.
8. Always speak in an even, soft tone.
9. Never express an opinion that might offend your guest.
10. Never lose your temper—at least, not in public.
11. Always look your best.
12. Never try to rescue yourself!

PROFESSOR KNIGHT WORD SEARCH

Professor Knight is a very old teacher at Ever After High. He grew up in a time when knights in shining armor were as famous as movie stars are today. He wishes those glory days would come again.

Can you find these words that can be used to describe knights? The words might be forward, backward, or diagonal.

MEDIEVAL   HELM
CHIVALRY   LANCE
COAT OF ARMS   GAUNTLETS
JOUSTING

A Y S L E D C M T P E E P P
R L T C R I O H Y B P K Z V
Q L N V U J A H E L M N U Q
A A F Z M P T O E M V H W G
L X J P K E O D U P M Y A N
G K J J Y C F U B L I U F V
N J U B P Y A F Z O N C V C
I P B B L W R Q N T W L Y V
T M J D S U M L L R I S Z Q
S F C F C L S E A S R H U M
U I Q A Y J T E O V D S V X
O M Q D Q S L A V E I D E M
J J A J N O H K X A H H O J
C T A P W N X N M S M T C H

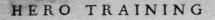

TOWER TALES

The story of a girl locked in a tower is one of the most common themes in fairytales.

For the modern reader, this tale can literally be about a girl physically locked in a stone tower, but it can also hold a deeper meaning. The tower is a symbol for something that imprisons you—something that holds you back or keeps you from doing what you want to do.

For example, in some parts of the world, girls aren't allowed to get an education. They yearn to be set free, to be allowed to learn.

The tower might be expectations. Darling wants to be an athlete, but she is locked in a tower of traditions. She yearns to be set free, too.

HERO TRAINING

Do you ever feel as if you're locked in a tower? What makes you feel this way? Write about your tower and how you'd like to be set free.

EVER AFTER
Royals!

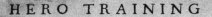

PEACOCK PRANCE

Daring Charming has a pet peacock named P-Hawk. Just like Daring, he's bursting with confidence. In fact, he loves to strut and prance around, fanning his tail feathers for all to admire.

Can you help P-Hawk prance his way through this maze at Ever After High? He needs to get from the swan pond to Daring, who is waiting with a bowl of peacock kibble.

HERO TRAINING

START HERE

FINISH

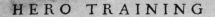

CASTLE QUEST

Darling, Daring, and Dexter grew up in a grand stone castle. To reach the castle, which is perched at the top of a mountain, they have to ride in a wobbly tram over deep ravines and sparkling glaciers. It's pretty cold up there, and lonely because it's so far away from the village.

HERO TRAINING

Living in a big, isolated castle can be lonely sometimes. When I am feeling lonely, here's what I like to do to cheer myself up:

If you were a princess and you could live in a castle, where would it be? Perhaps you like cold mountaintops, or maybe you prefer the beach, a flower-filled meadow, or a glistening lake. Using the art supplies of your choice, can you create a fantasy landscape around your castle? Don't forget to add details to the castle, too.

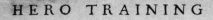

PRINCESS FOR A DAY #1

Why do we love stories about princesses? Is it because we all long to feel special? Do we want to be one of a kind? The center of attention? What do you think?

If you could be a princess for a day, what would you do? Would you enjoy yourself and relax? Or would you use your power to effect change? On the following pages, write about what you would do.

HERO TRAINING

PRINCESS FOR A DAY #2

Now that you've decided what kind of princess you'd be, how about designing your crown? Maybe it's a traditional crown with gemstones, or one with ornate patterns carved into it. Or maybe it's something more modern, with a headset so you can listen to music. You decide!

EVER AFTER
Royals!

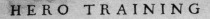

TROLL TOLLS

When the tram to Charming Castle is out of order, you have to walk up the steep, treacherous mountain trail. Along the way you will encounter trolls, who guard their bridges. They will ask you to pay a toll. Sometimes the toll is a coin, but other times it's a game. On this day, the trolls are in a riddling sort of mood.

To pass each bridge, you must unscramble words that have to do with the Charming family. Good luck.

HERO TRAINING

Bridge #1:
LODAARTTIIN _____

Bridge #2:
ALORYS _____

Bridge #3:
EESHOR _____

Bridge #4:
AELSSMD _____

Bridge #5:
EENRGTNSOIA _____

Answers: 1. traditional;
2. royals; 3. heroes;
4. damsels; 5. generations

DESIGN A POSTER

Rosabella Beauty, who is destined to be the hero of her own story, is still trying to persuade the Village of Book End that all boys, girls, and beasts are created equal. But she needs your help designing some posters, which she'll put up all over campus.

Using the art supplies of your choice, design some posters. What hexcellent slogans can you come up with?

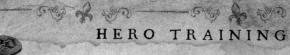

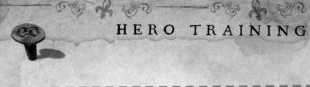

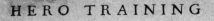

DEAR DIARY
✳ DARING ✳

At Ever After High, Daring is considered to be a perfect hero. He's handsome, brave, and bursting with confidence. He duels, jousts, and fights dragons without having to practice. He does everything perfectly. Girls swoon over him, and guys want to be him.

Pretend you are Daring. The day has ended, as it usually does, with you writing about how amazing and perfect you are. Try to capture Daring's confident voice. But on this day, something happened that made you feel a little less than perfect. What happened?

Dear Diary,

HERO TRAINING

RE
Write

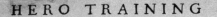

THRONEWORK ASSIGNMENT #5
HERO QUIZ

Heroes are all around us; they come in all shapes and genders, and from all kinds of backgrounds. Can you match the hero with his or her deed?

HERO TRAINING

1. Prince Charming
2. Beauty
3. Jack
4. Prince Charming
5. the Huntsman
6. a princess
7. Jill
8. Little Pig #3

a. kisses a frog and turns him into a prince

b. calls 911 after Jack breaks his crown

c. awakens Snow White with a kiss

d. ends the Beast's curse with true love

e. cuts through a wall of briars to save Sleeping Beauty

f. rescues Red Riding Hood

g. builds a house of bricks to thwart the Big Bad Wolf

h. trades a cow for magic beans that yield riches for him and his mother

Answers: 1. c or e, 2. d, 3. h, 4. c or e, 5. f, 6. a, 7. b, 8. g

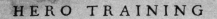

DARLING CHARMING'S DESTINY DO-OVER

Each character in Ever After High is part of a fairytale legacy, with a destiny that has been recorded in the Storybook of Legends.

Darling has been raised to believe that she must wait for her prince to arrive and rescue her, but she doesn't want to do that. She's trained herself to be an athlete, and she's ready for whatever adventure comes her way. So while she's not an official Rebel, she's certainly a secret rebel.

If you could rewrite the Storybook of Legends and give Darling a new ending to her story, what would you write?

HERO TRAINING

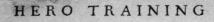

WRITE, IGNITE

Just like the characters in *A Semi-Charming Kind of Life*, you have a destiny. But as you know by now, your destiny is not written in a magical storybook. It is written by you!

Imagine that you are a hero. Your local newspaper has written an article about you. What was your heroic deed? Be sure to draw a picture of yourself.

LOCAL STUDENT BECOMES HERO

EVER AFTER
Royals!

EVER AFTER
Rebels

A HERO'S SELF-PORTRAIT

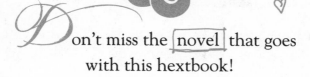

on't miss the novel that goes
with this hextbook!

Read **A Semi-Charming Kind of Life**
by Suzanne Selfors
to find out what destiny awaits
Darling Charming and
Dexter Charming!

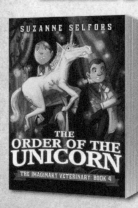